STORYTIME CLASSICS

A Little Princess

by Frances Hodgson Burnett

retold by Janet Allison Brown • illustrated by Graham Rust

Viking

VIKING
Published by the Penguin Group
Penguin Putnam Books for Young Readers, 345 Hudson Street, New York, New York 10014, U.S.A.
Penguin Books Ltd, 27 Wrights Lane, London W8 5TZ, England
Penguin Books Australia Ltd, Ringwood, Victoria, Australia
Penguin Books Canada Ltd, 10 Alcorn Avenue, Toronto, Ontario, Canada M4V 3B2
Penguin Books (N.Z.) Ltd, 182-190 Wairau Road, Auckland 10, New Zealand

Penguin Books Ltd, Registered Offices: Harmondsworth, Middlesex, England

First published in Great Britain by Breslich & Foss, 2001
Published simultaneously by Viking and Puffin Books,
divisions of Penguin Putnam Books for Young Readers, 2001

10 9 8 7 6 5 4 3 2 1

LIBRARY OF CONGRESS CATALOGING-IN-PUBLICATION DATA
Brown, Janet Allison.
A little princess / by Frances Hodgson Burnett ; illustrated by Graham
Rust ; re-told by Janet Allison Brown.
p.   cm.
Summary: Sara Crewe, a pupil at Miss Minchin's London school, is left in
poverty when her father dies but is later rescued by a mysterious
benefactor.
ISBN 0-670-89913-5 (hardcover) — ISBN 0-14-131203-3 (pbk.)
[1. Boarding schools—Fiction. 2. Schools—Fiction.
3. Orphans—Fiction. 4. London (England)—Fiction.] I. Rust, Graham, ill.
II. Burnett, Frances Hodgson, 1849–1924. Little princess. III. Title.
PZ7.B814815 Li 2001 [E]—dc21 00-011880

Printed in Belgium

Frances Hodgson Burnett
1849–1924

Frances Hodgson Burnett, who wrote this story, was born in England but went to live in America when she was sixteen. Three years later her first book was published, and she eventually wrote over forty novels, many of them for children. Her most famous books are *A Little Princess, The Secret Garden*, and *Little Lord Fauntleroy.*

Sara Crewe grew up in India with servants and every luxury. Her mother had died when she was young, but she was very close to her father, Captain Crewe, and they did everything together.

When Sara was seven, the Captain took her to
boarding school in England. On a dark winter's
day, their cab drew up outside Miss Minchin's
Select Seminary for Young Ladies.

Before he returned to India, Captain Crewe made sure that Sara had everything she needed. She had a pretty bedroom and sitting room of her own. She had a pony and a carriage. You might think, from this, that Sara would act very spoiled—but she didn't. She was thoughtful, kind, and good at her lessons.

At school, Sara had three special friends. They were not Lavinia or Jessie, or any of the other rich, pretty girls. The first was Emily, a beautiful doll that Captain Crewe had bought to keep Sara company. (Sara liked to believe that Emily was alive and really heard and understood.) The second was Ermengarde, an odd little girl who was not clever at all. And the third was Lottie, who was only four, had no mother, and cried a lot.

One day Sara found Becky, one of the young servants, fast asleep in her room. "Poor little girl," thought Sara. "She looks so tired."

Suddenly Becky woke up. "Please don't tell Miss Minchin!" she cried.

Of course, Sara did not tell Miss Minchin. Instead, she told Becky wonderful stories, and gave her meat pies and cakes. "I am only a little girl like you," said Sara. "It is only an accident that I am not you, and you are not me!"

Sara had a great imagination. One of her favorite "pretends" was that she was a princess. "I pretend I am a princess so that I can try and behave like one," she said.

Miss Minchin, the headmistress, always made a great fuss over Sara because she was so rich. On Sara's eleventh birthday, Miss Minchin threw a big party. Everyone was invited—even Becky the servant—and there were dozens of presents from Captain Crewe.

Everyone was having a lovely time, admiring the presents and eating cake, when terrible news arrived. Captain Crewe, Sara's beloved father, had lost all his money and died of a fever! Sara, one of the richest girls in India and England, was suddenly as poor as Becky.

Miss Minchin only liked rich girls. "Well, Sara," she said unkindly. "Now that you are poor you will have to make yourself useful!"

Sara's lovely things were taken away. She was given an attic room next to Becky's, and made to work as a servant. She wore old clothes and ran errands to the grocer. She carried laundry and taught the other girls their lessons.

But Sara still had her friends: Emily the doll, odd little Ermengarde, motherless Lottie— and Becky!

Sara was hungry and cold. She was tired and lonely. But she still had her imagination. She made friends with the rat that shared her attic, and told herself stories. Sometimes Ermengarde visited Sara to keep her company.

"Whatever comes," Sara thought, "cannot alter one thing. Even if I am dressed in rags and tatters, I can be a princess inside."

Sara was always hungry, so one day, when she was lucky enough to find a coin in the street, she ran to the baker and bought six buns. But when she came out of the shop, Sara noticed a beggar girl who looked even hungrier than she did.

Sara thought, "If I am a princess, I must share with others." So she gave the girl five of her buns.

"Well, I never!" said the baker, staring.

One morning, furniture began to arrive at the empty house next door. Shortly afterward, a pale man called Mr. Carrisford moved in. He had lived in India for many years, but now he was very ill.

He brought with him an Indian servant called Ram Dass, and a little pet monkey.

Ram Dass noticed Sara almost immediately. He saw how kind she was, and how much she suffered.

Ram Dass told Mr. Carrisford all about Sara's kindness and generosity, and together they planned a special surprise for her....

The next morning, Sara awoke and this is what
she saw: a blazing fire in the grate, a soft rug
on the floor, a table full of breakfast dishes,

blankets on the bed, and a pile of books. On the
books was a note: "To the little girl in the attic.
From a friend."

What Sara did not know was that Mr. Carrisford was her father's friend, and he was looking for her. He was ill with worry because he could not find her.

What Mr. Carrisford did not know, was that the little servant who lived in the attic next door, to whom he had already been so kind, was the very girl he was searching for!

One day, Mr. Carrisford's monkey leaped over the rooftops and into Sara's attic. "I must take you back!" said Sara, cuddling the monkey. She crept out of school and rang the bell next door. Ram Dass took her straight in to see Mr. Carrisford.

As soon as Mr. Carrisford saw her, he knew who she was. "It is the child!" he cried, and tears ran down his face. Then he told Sara that he had been her father's friend, and that he wanted to take care of her. "I have looked everywhere for you," he said, "and all the time you were right next door!"

So Sara came to live with Mr. Carrisford—or Uncle Tom, as she called him. He bought her everything she wanted and came to love her very much. Becky came to live with them too, and Ermengarde and Lottie came to visit whenever they wanted.

But Sara did not forget her days in rags. She went back to the baker where she had bought the buns, and bought lots of food for the poor. "I know what it is like to be hungry," said the little princess.